Acting Edition

I0741563

The People Before the Park

by Keith Josef Adkins

ꟾꟾSAMUEL FRENCHꟾꟾ

FOR PRODUCTION INQUIRIES

UNITED STATES AND CANADA
info@concordtheatricals.com
1-866-979-0447

UNITED KINGDOM AND EUROPE
licensing@concordtheatricals.co.uk
020-7054-7298

Each title is subject to availability from Concord Theatricals Corp., depending upon country of performance. Please be aware that THE PEOPLE BEFORE THE PARK may not be licensed by Concord Theatricals Corp. in your territory. Professional and amateur producers should contact the nearest Concord Theatricals Corp. office or licensing partner to verify availability.

MUSIC AND THIRD-PARTY MATERIALS USE NOTE

IMPORTANT BILLING AND CREDIT REQUIREMENTS

THE PEOPLE BEFORE THE PARK was originally commissioned by Epic Theatre Ensemble in New York City. It won the Premiere Stages New Play Festival, and was subsequently produced by Premiere Stages (John J. Wooten, Producing Artistic Director) at Kean University in September 2015. The production was directed by John J. Wooten, with scenic design by Patrick Rizzotti, lighting design by Brant Thomas Murray, sound design by Janie Bullard, costume design by Karen Lee Hart, and props by Helen Tewksbury. The production stage manager was Dale Smallwood. The cast was as follows:

STEPHEN VAN CLEEF . . . . Billy Eugene Jones

JONAS VAN CLEEF . . . . W. Tre Davis

BRIDGET DONNELY . . . . Bridget Gabbe

PHOEBE FERNANDES LEWIS . . . . Michelle Wilson

MARION LEWIS . . . . Shane Taylor

MATHIUS FRACKENHINGER . . . . Andy Truschinksi

THE PEOPLE BEFORE THE PARK was subsequently produced at the University of Iowa's Mainstage Theater in March 2021. The production was directed by Jade King Carroll, with scenic design by Tobin Griffin, lighting design by Bryon Winn, sound design by Huda Al-Aithan, costume design by Loyce Arthur, and dialect coaching by Crystal Marie Stewart. The production stage manager was Brillan Qi-Bell. The cast was as follows:

STEPHEN VAN CLEEF . . . . Branden Shaw

JONAS VAN CLEEF . . . . Steven Antoine Willis

BRIDGET DONNELY . . . . Kate Anderson

PHOEBE FERNANDES LEWIS . . . . Britny J. Horton

MARION LEWIS . . . . Octavius Lanier

MATHIUS FRACKENHINGER . . . . Aaron Kruger

CHARACTERS

STEPHEN VAN CLEEF – Black, 42, rough-edged, a New Yorker, oysterman

JONAS VAN CLEEF – His son, Black, 22, daydreamer, a New Yorker, artist

BRIDGET DONNELY – Irish, 18, curious, born in Ireland, laborer

PHOEBE FERNANDES LEWIS – Black, 40, New Yorker, daughter of Haitians, teacher

MARION LEWIS – Black, 42, a New Yorker, husband of Phoebe, shoe merchant

MATHIUS FRACKENHINGER – 22, born in Germany, police officer

SETTING

New York City. 85th Street, between 7th and 8th Avenues – Seneca Village

The playing areas include: front of the one-story Van Cleef house, inside the Lewis' two-story house, the A.M.E. Zion Cemetery.

A large pile of oyster shells stands next to the Van Cleef house.

TIME

Summer 1856.

AUTHOR'S NOTES

On a screen – at the top of the show – the following should be seen:

Central Park was erected and these people were affected.

Note on dialects

Mid-nineteenth-century New Yorkers dropped the "r" in words. Example: oyster is oystah, horsecar is hawsecah, and water is wautah. A word like again is pronounced a-gayne.

Mid-19th-century New Yorker dialect is not heavy like the accents of modern-day Brooklyn, Bronx, Staten Island, etc. It was softer due to the British legacy of the City.

The Black characters in this play are not southern. Their culture and linguistics have not been shaped by slavery in the south. The Black characters in this play are sixth-generation New Yorkers.

Note on the world of the play

This is a brutal New York City. There is nothing earnest about it or its inhabitants. The production should resonate with the raw, brutal realness of 19th-century New York City.

ACT ONE

Scene One

(The front of the Van Cleef house. Thursday. Early morning.)

*(***STEPHEN*** lays a tin slab onto the roof. He also sings fast and loudly while he works.)*

STEPHEN.
DRINK TO ME ONLY WITH THINE EYES
AND I WILL PLEDGE WITH MINE.
OR LEAVE A KISS WITHIN THE CUP...

(He hears someone approaching. Grabs knife.)

Who's there?! If you don't shout your name, I'll throw this knife right through your skull! I've got good aim, too. And blood doesn't scare me.

*(***MATHIUS*** enters, in police uniform. His left hand stuffed curiously into his pocket.)*

I told you to shout your name before you walk up, Mathius! I don't like surprises or visitors. You walk up without warning, you might get knived.

MATHIUS. *(A bit nervous.)* Ja, I forget these things. So much to remember with you. Guten Morgen, Mister Van Cleef.

STEPHEN. Yeah yeah! Someone's been prowling around lately. Knocked over a barrel of molasses over at William Pease's and broke his window. He's a middling grocer for certain but can't afford to lose any goods. Know anything about that? Because if you do...

MATHIUS. Nein, I don't. But rascals everywhere you go in city. Ja? Always rascals.

STEPHEN. Everybody knows those Council bastards want our land for that Park – so if they or anybody come over here they will get knived, for certain! So shout your name.

MATHIUS. I brought you some vinegar. Had extra. Lots of mosquitos lately.

STEPHEN. Vinegar? *(A bit ungrateful.)* You need to stop bringing me things every time I see you. It's bothersome. *(Then.)* Put it down over there, son.

MATHIUS. *(Puts down bottle.)* Do you need help with roof? Is it bad?

STEPHEN. That rainstorm left its mark. Water dripped all night. In my face, mouth. Lucky I didn't drown in my sleep. These tin sheets should do the trick. Did your roofs hold?

> *(He steps down from the ladder. He crosses to his oyster cart. Begins to prep it with nearby gloves, bucket, knife, tongs, and a small block of ice.)*

MATHIUS. The rain not kind to our roofs. A few crash in. No necks broke. Ha-ha.

STEPHEN. Those shanties you all live in aren't worth the shit on my boot. No reason to live like squatters. Told y'all that. Make your home a home. You live like rats in the woods.

MATHIUS. It is fine. Not enough wages to move to Bloomingdale Road quite yet. But one day I will I hope.

STEPHEN. A few of y'all pigs got loose a-gain a day back. So all is *not* fine. Huh?

MATHIUS. The pigs come back? Mensch! I try to mention to the others –

STEPHEN. They come here and ate my cabbage. Shit everywhere too. *(Points.)* Tell your Germans, keep their pigs away from here, or I'll strangle 'em and sell the meat on Orange Street. *(Then.)* Don't stand there gawking. Be useful and hand me that basket.

MATHIUS. *(Hands basket to him.)* You sing like you happy. When I walk up.

STEPHEN. That's what I sometimes do. Wake, sing. Mind my business. A man is allowed that, isn't he? I reckon wherever you go in the world. China, Prussia, Calcutta, a man wakes up and does what he wants.

MATHIUS. *(Joking.)* Sing again about kisses I might have to put you in jail for indecency.

STEPHEN. *(More serious.)* If you're going to put me in jail, put. Indecency has never scared me. I might scare *it*, but it never scares me. I once lived in Five Points. Put my knuckle to many of faces.

MATHIUS. *(Apologetic.)* Entschuldigung, Mister Van Cleef. I'm only having the fun with you.

STEPHEN. What do you want, Mathius? Sounds like you're good with the new job. Ready to put people in jail for singing.

(Goes back to oyster cart.)

MATHIUS. I have new uniform. You like?

STEPHEN. *(Surveys.)* Kind of big in the shoulders if you ask me. Looks like it's eating you and that's not a compliment you need to hold on to.

*(**MATHIUS** coughs a little.)*

STEPHEN. I see you still have that cough. The last time I saw you, you were coughing. Sounded like tuberculosis. I lost two cousins to that White Plague. Killed them in a week.

MATHIUS. It's not in chest, only throat. But I will not die I hope. Just got uniform. Ha-ha.

STEPHEN. Well, it's swampy up here. Got to keep your throat covered at night. That reservoir don't help your cause either. Told you that. You don't listen.

MATHIUS. The reservoir is not bad. Nice to look. It's like big ship on land –

STEPHEN. – Yorkville Reservoir *is* bad. The Common Council just had to put it up here with us Negroes. Probably did it to kill us off. No telling what poisons coming from it –

MATHIUS. The council does what it likes, Mister Van Cleef. But the city grows. New things must go somewhere –

STEPHEN. I have nothing a-gainst new things, or where they go. But seems to me the city's always putting *new* things where Negroes and poor people live –

MATHIUS. This is not true –

STEPHEN. Why are you defending this city? When you first got here you despised it. Said it smelled like puke and shit. Now all you do is defend –

MATHIUS. I don't defend –

STEPHEN. They're threatening to turn this area into a park. A Central Park. I'm certain you know about that. And who lives here? Negroes and poor people. You don't see that, you're blind as a dead man – too much water in the air will give anybody a *cough*. That's all I'm saying, It'll be the end of your young life, whether you got a new uniform or not.

(Noticing **MATHIUS** *hiding his hand.)* What's wrong with your hand?

MATHIUS. Got jostled by a few of the coppers at work.

(Brief silence.)

STEPHEN. Jostled? You screw one of their whores? They'll slice off your jollystick for that.

MATHIUS. For living up here.

STEPHEN. Up here? *(Slight pause.)* Near the Negroes I reckon?

MATHIUS. They put my hand in hot water. To clean off the black, they say.

STEPHEN. Let me see.

*(***MATHIUS*** shows.)*

Bloody! You standing here with a burned hand and have said nothing?

(Grabs a small jar of pine sap.)

MATHIUS. They call this place Nigger Village, Mister Van Cleef.

*(***STEPHEN*** applies sap to his hand. ***MATHIUS*** winces.)*

STEPHEN. I advised you about these coppers. Mayor Fernando Wood governs them. He belongs to that corrupt Tammany Hall and they run everything. Tricked these Irish boys into thinking the city cares for 'em so they can use 'em. Now they tricked you.

MATHIUS. I am not a dummkopf, Mister Van Cleef. Just not happy with things I learn.

STEPHEN. Well, most coppers are filth. They do whatever Mayor Wood tells and he's a thug. That's printed in the *Times* and the *Tribune*. I'd find another job.

MATHIUS. What other? Sweep chimneys again? I don't know. *(Uncertain himself.)*

STEPHEN. You can make a decent wage on the docks too. Lifting sugarcane, cotton.

MATHIUS. Everybody seek wage on docks. I have uniform. This respektvoll job.

STEPHEN. Respectful? I saw three coppers cut a man on Bowery just last week. Watched him bleed near-death, then pissed on him. Just because he refused to step out of their way. But if that's respectful to you... Look... I got to get to the river for my oystahs.

    (He goes back to the oyster cart.)

Thanks for the vinegar.

    *(**MATHIUS** begins to exit.)*

...If you see any rascals causing trouble, make sure to let me know.

MATHIUS. *(Wanting to say more, quietly.)* Mister Van Cleef, I want –

STEPHEN. *(Uninterested.)* What is it Mathius?

MATHIUS. *(Brief pause, deciding not to say anything.)* Guten Tag, Mister Van Cleef.

    *(**MATHIUS** exits.)*

    *(**STEPHEN** packs his cart, singing.)*

STEPHEN.
DRINK TO ME ONLY WITH THINE EYES

Scene Two

(The front of the Van Cleef house. Thursday. Early evening.)

*(**JONAS** draws on paper as **STEPHEN**, bare-chested, washes his upper body.)*

STEPHEN. That Paddy picks up my oystahs and said they smelled like dead fish. He's lucky I didn't cut his throat.

JONAS. I'd say he *is* lucky, Papa. He and his throat. Real lucky.

STEPHEN. How long have I been selling oystahs on Fourteenth Street, Jonas? I fry them, pickle, serve them raw in half shell. They never soured a stomach. Even when I was selling on Bleecker Street, nobody lamented. Not even that woman who bought my oystahs but refused to touch my black hand. I make the best oystahs in New York City. Better than Thomas Downing himself.

JONAS. Thomas Downing? You're loony, Papa. You don't mean *that*.

STEPHEN. You have issue with me being better than Thomas Downing? I make oystahs better than anybody I know. From here to Boston to Barbados.

JONAS. It's just... He's got a fancy eating place near Wall Street. Across from the Exchange.

STEPHEN. So what!

JONAS. Queen Victoria even ate his oystahs and gave him a watch in appreciation.

STEPHEN. Nobody cares that he's across from the Exchange or what Queen Victoria gave. That lunatic queen will give anything to anybody. She's a lunatic. *(Then.)* Sounds like you prefer him as your father than me. That's what it sounds like.

JONAS. That's not what I prefer –

STEPHEN. I know what he's got, Jonas! He's a Negro, he's rich, so what. If you like *salt*, he's the perfect man for you. I'm talking about this Paddy insulting my oystahs.

JONAS. Yes. The Paddy and the oystahs. Pardon.

STEPHEN. Is that a tone? You're not too old for a whack.

JONAS. There's no tone.

STEPHEN. *(Tossing him sack of money.)* That Paddy standing there with holes in his pants. Teeth about as black as dirt. I was giving him something to eat like a gentleman, and he gonna say that my oystahs taste like dead fish. *I* may taste like *dead fish* but my oystahs are top notch. Got the cuts on my hand to prove it.

JONAS. *(Slightly patronizing.)* You've got a lot of cuts. More than most. *(Counting small bag of money.)*

STEPHEN. No one has *ever* insulted my oystahs. And I've been in the oystah business since I was twelve.

JONAS. *(Re: money.)* You sold a lot. It was a good day. You need to rest. I boiled the sheets. Got those rum stains out. You can sleep on something clean. You seem restless.

STEPHEN. What I care about clean sleeping? I'm going to the river to get more oystahs so I can go back and sell them. That's what I'm going to do. A pocket fat with coins is how you survive New York. I had a good day, yes, but it could've been better. That Paddy's lucky he's still breathing. He's lucky he still has a throat. I'll rest on clean sheets when I'm dead and buried.

JONAS. Okay. Dead and buried.

(He picks up paper and draws on it.)

STEPHEN. *(Noticing hanging undergarments.)* Jonas! Jonas!!

JONAS. What is it now, Papa?

STEPHEN. I asked you *not* to hang these drawers out front. Hang them in back. Them ladies at A.M.E. Zion spent a month pulling down my drawers...

JONAS. A *day*. That was all it was.

STEPHEN. If I had my way, I'd hang them anywhere I please. Walk around in nothing but my naked skin if I prefer. But I don't want them touching my drawers a-gain. Hang them in back.

JONAS. *(Joking.)* Maybe it's not your drawers they want to touch. Maybe it's something else.

STEPHEN. Watch your step, gambler. You're about to lose your money and your life.

> *(He steps toward* **JONAS**, *playfully threatening him.)*

JONAS. *(Changing subject.)* Papa... Saturday I go to my drawing lesson –

STEPHEN. Am I doing this by myself? Grab these drawers! Grab!

JONAS. *(Crosses to him.)* We can invite a guest...to see us work. I want you to see me work –

STEPHEN. Did you speak to your boss at the hotel about more wages? I asked you this morning. The rain punched holes in the roof. We need extra wages to cover the costs of fixing.

JONAS. I forgot. I'll ask tomorrow.

STEPHEN. You better. They've got you boys over there waiting on tables all day and paying you pebbles. I don't like anyone swindling you, Jonas.

JONAS. Did you hear what I said? I can invite a guest, to my art lesson –

STEPHEN. I have no time to sit in some parlor looking at bloody pictures with some fancy people, drinking tea and the like. They'll probably make me stand in the back anyway. Near the kitchen. I don't stand in the back for anybody.

JONAS. You won't have to be in the back. The guests sit near the front.

STEPHEN. With them white dandy folks? I rather get bludgeoned.

JONAS. You'll be able to see what I do for once. My landscapes and portraits –

STEPHEN. I don't want to speak on this drawing stuff. You don't need to be losing any sleep over it either. When I was your age I had a steady job, a steady mind. That's what I want for you. You keep trying to climb too high in this city, boy, and you're liable to fall and break your back. *(Then.)* You're looking at me like you don't understand.

JONAS. *(Acquiescing.)* I understand.

      *(**BRIDGET** enters, hovers, a bit nervous.)*

STEPHEN. What are you doing over here, girl? Don't tell me you're trying to get free food already? Day isn't even over yet.

JONAS. *(Disapproving.)* Papa.

BRIDGET. Just saying hello. That's all it is.

STEPHEN. You expect me to believe you're here for a simple greeting?

BRIDGET. Yes. I like you to believe it.

STEPHEN. Tell your mother if she wants some oystahs she'll have to pay for it this time.

BRIDGET. She says if she can have some on credit 'til Sunday, she'll make you a fresh oat cake.

STEPHEN. Your mother paid on credit for the last two weeks. Oystah eating isn't free. I'm not some **Colored dandy** from downtown, handing out everything I earn to charity. I own this property, but that's about all I got.

JONAS. Bridget just wants a few. We can manage a few.

STEPHEN. Jonas, I know you want to keep feeding this girl. But she has a papa. He's the one supposed to pour porridge in her pail, not me. He's a working man, isn't he?

BRIDGET. He spent his week's pay down at a dance hall in Five Points.

STEPHEN. Speak up, girl! I can't hear you! He what?

BRIDGET. He spent his wages in Five Points. A bloody lip and a black eye is what he come home with. Nothing more.

STEPHEN. Well, it sounds like the whores of Five Points having better luck than you.

JONAS. Papa! The mouth on you sometimes. *(Frustrated.)* Bloody!

STEPHEN. Boy, those whores are holding on to pots of gold and I'm not talking about what's under their skirts! *(To* **BRIDGET**.*)* Tell your Ma she pays what she owes, she gets oystahs. That's how things work in this city. You give, you get.

BRIDGET. Yes sir.

STEPHEN. Jonas, hang those drawers in back while I'm gone. Did you hear me? Hang 'em!

  (He exits.)

JONAS. *(Handing her oysters.)* Take these.

BRIDGET. Jonas. No. Mister Van Cleef said…

JONAS. He doesn't mean half of what comes from his mouth. Take it.

(She does.)

BRIDGET. The lady I clean chamber pots for didn't pay me wage today. Said she found a crumb bug in her stockings. Blamed me for it. First time I'm accused of spreading crumb bugs.

JONAS. People like to blame others for their "dirt." That's the way of the world.

BRIDGET. She looked through my hair for 'em. Fingers through me scalp. Scratching up blood.

JONAS. Do you want me to go over to speak to the lady? I will. Clobber her if you want. Tie her up so you can clobber her too. Scratch up blood from her scalp.

BRIDGET. Like you whacked the boy who threw the rock at me?

JONAS. Yeah. Like that.

BRIDGET. Perhaps the morrow. But that's sweet of ya.

(They laugh.)

JONAS. I'm happy to see you. I mean I'm always happy –

(**BRIDGET** *picks up Jonas's drawing. Admires it.)*

BRIDGET. You always make things look better than they really are.

JONAS. Didn't realize I was doing that.

BRIDGET. I better go.

JONAS. Your papa's not going to look for you here.

BRIDGET. Don't want Mister Van Cleef to catch me. Might throw a rock.

JONAS. If he throws a rock, I'll throw it back. Hit him right in the nose. Crack it. Break it!

STEPHEN. *(Re-entering.)* Jonas! Are those my oystahs she got?! Are those my oystahs?!

JONAS. We can't let neighbors go hungry.

STEPHEN. Bloody, boy! Well...if you're going to give her some, give enough to fill her stomach. Dont want her to starve and I'm jailed for my lack of kindness.

> *(**JONAS** gives more.)*

BRIDGET. Thank you, Mister Van Cleef. You're an angel man. God's gonna bless your teeth and toes.

> *(She leaves in a hurry.)*

JONAS. That was good of you. You're good sometimes.

STEPHEN. Yeah, I'm good. As long as I'm handing over everything I own! *(Grabs oyster basket.)* Now hang those drawers out back. Hurry, Jonas!

Scene Three

(A few hours later. In front of the Van Cleef house.)

*(**JONAS** draws on paper. **PHOEBE** sits, waving away mosquitoes. **MARION** paces.)*

MARION. This vandalizing spooked the Stewarts. First somebody broke their windows, cracked their front door, then poured kerosene in their garden. Mayor Wood, somebody, is certainly trying to unnerve our wits. This park they want to build is turning everybody into savages.

PHOEBE. They were already savages if you want my opinion.

MARION. Well, we don't want your opinion, Phoebe. It's dangerous.

PHOEBE. Sometimes a dangerous thought is the medicine people need, Marion.

JONAS. Someone poured kerosene? In their garden?

MARION. You didn't smell that this morning? What are you and Stephen doing over here? Smoking opium? That odor was strong enough to knock out a pig. A half a day it lingered and you didn't smell it?

JONAS. I smelled something. Thought it was steamboat exhaust –

MARION. It was kerosene and whoever poured it was ready to set that garden aflame.

PHOEBE. Lucky Mister Stewart ran off whoever it was. Negroes always have to worry about being burned out.

MARION. Calm yourself, Phoebe. You're going to upset the heavens.

PHOEBE. And that's a problem?

MARION. How soon do you expect Stephen to return, Jonas? We need to speak to him.

JONAS. If he catches the tide, he'll stay late on the river for better oystahing.

PHOEBE. We can't wait until then. We need to take to the streets and make some noise.

MARION. If we go out and riot we could lose everything, Phoebe. Why can't you see that? No place for fugitives to harbor. We've been a safe haven for runaways for years and that will be over. Let's attempt the civilized route first.

PHOEBE. Mister Stewart said someone followed him from the Common Council last week. After he demanded the full value of his home. And now they're kerosening gardens. If this isn't a reason to riot, then I'm a fool and lock me away.

MARION. These people will lock you away for being less than a fool and you know it!

JONAS. Was Mister Stewart hurt?

MARION. All I know is the Council gave him five hundred dollars to move from his property. The value's a thousand. That's not much for a family of ten. I told him I can make them shoes to carry them over, but they need more than that.

JONAS. Maybe I should give 'em some oystahs.

PHOEBE. That would be decent of you. But it won't remedy the hate hurled at us every day.

MARION. Jonas, a group of us are gathering tomorrow at A.M.E. Zion. We're putting together an affidavit. Our lawyer says a legal, *group* effort may have greater impact. First, the council says we have to leave Seneca and now they expect us to accept these small monies. We deserve our values like any other white man in New York and we won't be threatened because we demand it.

PHOEBE. A stranger looked into Mary Jackson's window last night.

JONAS. *(Not believing it.)* What?! Are you certain?

MARION. Phoebe, I asked you not to share that indecency.

PHOEBE. She was putting on bedding clothes. Her bosoms exposed and more. I believe it was one of those vandalizers. Women aren't safe and I'm going to say something about it.

MARION. The Common Council, the coppers, the mayor, somebody's trying to scare us now. Mister Jackson said he's considering taking the money and moving to Weeksville in Brooklyn. Folks keep thinking like that we won't have anybody in Seneca to fight.

PHOEBE. *(Waving bugs.)* These mosquitoes are trying to kill me.

JONAS. *(Hands her vial.)* Here's some vinegar. When Papa returns I'll tell him you paid a visit.

PHOEBE. Marion, this boy is shooing us away like these bugs.

JONAS. I have an art lesson and I want to be prepared –

PHOEBE. Drawing a woman's thigh? That's not a lesson I ever taught.

MARION. We're worried, Jonas. About our homes. Our future. *Yours*. We need you to start thinking like a man and not a boy. This is serious.

JONAS. I believe it's serious, Marion. But it's only a threat.

PHOEBE. That's a matter worth debating –

MARION. Stephen's disregard for everything is not his most favorable attribute. So don't you acquire it too.

STEPHEN. *(Entering with cage.)* Well somebody gut me like a whale! God must have blown his bloody trumpet to send Marion and Phoebe Lewis over here. What's the occasion? Jesus coming and you collecting offerings? All I got is an oystah. But these lovelies may be big enough for the Messiah's appetite. What you think?

MARION. Hello Stephen. How are you?

JONAS. *(Grabbing some of* **STEPHEN**'s *gear.)* I didn't expect you until sunset.

STEPHEN. High tide came in early! Almost like omen. *(Then.)* So why are you at my house and when are you leaving?

> *(He begins to remove his boots, pants.)*

PHOEBE. Stephen, we're here about the vandalizing. The Stewarts are moving out of Seneca. His crops were kerosened after Mister Stewart asked for the value of his house.

STEPHEN. Well, tell them to take them roosters. Let them torture somebody else's sleep.

PHOEBE. Roosters? He's a lunatic.

STEPHEN. Jonas, go back and get me some soap.

MARION. Stephen, we're being intimidated! A-gain!

> *(***JONAS*** exits.)*

> *(***MARION*** notices ***STEPHEN*** disrobing.)*

You are undressing in front of my wife, man.

STEPHEN. Maybe if you undressed in front of her she wouldn't be looking this way.

PHOEBE. You vulgar –

Somebody should cut out your –

MARION. Stephen, you will not refer to Phoebe in that manner – Now we're trying to have a civilized discussion with you –

MARION. We know the Council offered you monies for this house. We're gathering at A.M.E. Zion tomorrow and we want you to meet the lawyer, sign the affidavit. Help us with this.

(**JONAS** *returns with soap.*)

STEPHEN. Hand me that soap, Jonas.

MARION. Stephen, everything we do as a people has a bearing on those slaves in the South. From the time we wake until we sleep and every moment in between. Our lives aren't just our lives. They're collateral for the Negro race. Your wife Susie knew that.

PHOEBE. It's like preaching to a wall.

MARION. This vandalizing is just the beginning. Destroying our crops. What next?! Flood us out? The more numbers we have to fight the council, the better.

PHOEBE. Love, let's go.

MARION. (*Frustrated.*) You always vanish when it's not easy, Stephen.

(**MARION** *and* **PHOEBE** *exit.*)

STEPHEN. Fire up that kettle for me. I stink.

JONAS. This park... Perhaps there is something to fret over –

STEPHEN. If Mayor Wood tries to take my home or land, they'll have me to deal with.

JONAS. But somebody poured kerosene in the Stewarts' garden –

STEPHEN. Why are you repeating their concerns? You sound like a parrot. And what's that in your hand? Not enough light to be scratching on paper today.

JONAS. Papa...don't you want to help –

STEPHEN.   Saw Mister Mohammad on Bloomingdale Road. Sold me some curry and cinnamon. Said they came all the way from his home in Calcutta. Let's say we try the curry and see if it's good enough for my customers. Because if it's good enough for Calcutta, it's good enough for New York.

Scene Four

(The A.M.E. Zion Cemetery.)

(Dusk.)

(**JONAS** *and* **BRIDGET** *sit.* **JONAS** *holds a paper with a drawing on it.)*

BRIDGET. You promised. Show it! Show it, Jonas. Or I will bite ye!

JONAS. *(Flirtatious.)* Bite? With your teeth? Where you want to bite me?

BRIDGET. Don't know. Wherever it hurts the most.

JONAS. I can find a place but it's not pain I want to feel from you.

BRIDGET. Ssh. What was that?

JONAS. *(Nervous.)* Where? I don't hear anything. What?

BRIDGET. Behind that headstone. Something's there. I swear it!

JONAS. *(Teasing.)* Aw, it's a dead member of the great A.M.E. Zion. We're disturbing his eternal peace. He'll get over it.

BRIDGET. Don't fool, Jonas. I imagine a dead hand's gonna come out of the ground and pull me down into the bones and worms.

JONAS. The A.M.E. Zions don't turn into bones and worms. They stay well suited throughout eternity. Well mannered too. Besides, I'll protect you.

BRIDGET. You jumped yerself. I may have to protect you.

JONAS. Okay, but only if you bite me first. And then let me bite you.

BRIDGET. I just... I don't want anyone to ever... This is our place, you know –

JONAS. They have to be looking for us to find us, Bridget. Told you that. *(Then, probing.)* Who scratched your lip? Looked like you were hit.

BRIDGET. *(Evading.)* It's nothing. Did it at work, scrubbing. I'm such a butterfingers.

JONAS. I saw your lip the other day –

BRIDGET. It happened at work. Alright? *(Then.)* What drawing are you carrying with you today? Can I see?

JONAS. You won't make a face or run off? Because if you make a face...

BRIDGET. Is it that horrible then?

> *(**JONAS** shows her. It's a young woman. Silence.)*

JONAS. My teacher says it's the third best. There's a man in the class who studied in Berlin. He's the first. And next is her daughter. Well, because it's her daughter but she's really not good. My teacher says the lines and colors are my most favorable skill.

BRIDGET. Whose face is it?

JONAS. Yours. Your face.

BRIDGET. Mine then? This?

JONAS. I worked on it all night but you don't have to like it for that cause –

BRIDGET. Didn't know me eyes were so sad.

JONAS. Sometimes. But that's alright. Everyone's allowed to be sad.

BRIDGET. Me look awful poor in the cheeks. Not like those plump dandy girls I see riding the horsecar.

JONAS. Hawsecah. Not "horsecar." Hawsecah. You still say it funny. *(Mocking her:)* "Horsecar."

BRIDGET. The Irish do a lot things funny I reckon, and people draw such horrible pictures of us. I saw a pamphlet on the street where someone drew us like we were half animal. Had a tail like we mated with rats, and its teeth were dripping with spit and blood –

JONAS. I didn't do a half animal... A rat...

BRIDGET. Why *did* you do it?

JONAS. I... Um... I just wanted to –

BRIDGET. It's quite fine. Especially the lines and colors. Especially that.

JONAS. My teacher says there's passage to Paris next month. Said she'd help pay if I wanted to go and study there.

BRIDGET. *(Jealous.)* Your teacher has a mouth full of sweetness for ye, doesn't she?

JONAS. She's just kind. She even wants me to go to Pfaff's after our Saturday lesson.

BRIDGET. What's Pfaff? Sounds fancy.

JONAS. It's a bar downtown on Bleeker Street. She wears her husband's trousers when she goes. She says men and a few women come and talk about politics and the general art of life. She meets all types there. There's a writer she met. Whitman is his name. He wrote a book called *Leaves and Grass*, about life in New York.

BRIDGET. Can't say I've heard of it.

JONAS. She says he's quite the gentleman but obscene.

BRIDGET. Obscene?

JONAS. A mary. He has a male companion. They hold hands inside the bar.

Paris, Pfaff's. The world is much larger than we imagine. The thought overwhelms me.

BRIDGET. Is this what you want for yerself? To go places and talk about the general art of life?

JONAS. I just want to know about everything. Not to be afraid of it. To breathe it in, breathe it out. I want to be able to see everyone, everything, and draw it all with truth. Kindness. Like I'm alive just to protect it. Is that wrong to you?

BRIDGET. ...I reckon this oat cake won't be a match for all of that.

(She pulls a cake from cloth.)

JONAS. You have your mother's oat cake? And with berries. Can I eat it now?

BRIDGET. No. You're forbidden at the moment. *(Then, playfully.)* Yes. Eat.

JONAS. *(Eating.)* What happened to your lip? You can tell me.

BRIDGET. ...I miss Ireland, Jonas. I miss me cousins. The rain and hills. Me mamo singing "Molly Malone" when I couldn't sleep. Me father drinks something awful since we got here. Rages and screams. Me mother begs almost every day. On the road sometimes; to people just passing by. It was bad for us in Galway, but here they call you ugly for it. A scut.

JONAS. I don't think you're ugly.

BRIDGET. No. You draw a nice and honest picture. I know I'm not much but I thank God that ye see me. You got so many other things you could see.

JONAS. So... Are you going to bite me now? I'm ready for the bite.

BRIDGET. Not certain a scut should be biting some dandy going off to Paris.

JONAS. You can go with me and we can bite each other far away from this place.

> *(They smile, lean in to kiss. Something rustles.)*

BRIDGET. What's that?

JONAS. Another dead member of the A.M.E. Zion. They like what they're seeing.

BRIDGET. I better go. Me da' may come looking. Thank ye for the drawing. For keeping me around in yer mind.

> *(**BRIDGET** quickly exits as lights fade on **JONAS** to reveal an eavesdropping and unhappy **STEPHEN**.)*

Scene Five

(Friday. Very early morning.)

(Lights up on the Van Cleefs' yard.)

(The sound of dozens of feisty pigs is heard in the near distance.)

*(***STEPHEN***, in his drawers [a bottle of rum stuck in the pocket], holds large stick.)*

STEPHEN. Jonas! Jonas! Wake up! *(To pigs.)* I will roast your guts for dinner. Jonas! Wake up!!

(A sleepy **JONAS** *enters, also in his drawers.)*

They're coming! Hear that? They're coming up the bluff. Don't you hear them?

JONAS. Who? It's early.

STEPHEN. They're coming! They're passing the reservoir right now. Listen! Listen!!

JONAS. *(Getting it.)* Pigs?

STEPHEN. No, *pirates*! Yes, the pigs! Pigs!! Cover the garden before they eat up everything we have!

JONAS. *(Concerned.)* Papa. You sound like you have a fever.

STEPHEN. Cover the garden like I said!

*(***JONAS*** *stares at* ***STEPHEN***, *confused.)*

What are you standing there?! Find something!

JONAS. What should I use? There's nothing out here!

STEPHEN. Use the sheets off the beds. Go on, boy!

JONAS. But I just washed them.

STEPHEN. Use the damned bloody sheets, Jonas! They're almost here!

(**JONAS** *goes in the house. The pigs are closer. A nearby dog barks.*)

STEPHEN. They're near Widow Henderson's yard! That's her dog barking. That's her old crickety dog! Hurry up, Jonas!!

(**JONAS** *returns with two large sheets.*)

JONAS. Do you see them yet?

STEPHEN. They're close!!! Must be twenty of them. Cover everything!

(**JONAS** *covers the garden.*)

(*The sound of the pig herd gets closer.*)

Bring it on, **swine-makers**! I'm ready for you! (*Then.*) You ready to split their heads open, Jonas?

JONAS. (*Indifferent.*) I reckon.

STEPHEN. Grab that stick. I'm ready to see blood!

(**JONAS** *grabs stick and joins* **STEPHEN** *who appears primed to fight something more sinister.*)

They're trying to take what's ours, Jonas. We can't let them take it.

JONAS. (*Concerned.*) Yes sir.

STEPHEN. Come on, **swine-makers**! We're going to bloody your bloody faces until we see blood!

(**STEPHEN** *and* **JONAS** *are in position.*)

(*Sticks in the air. After a moment, the pig herd bypasses.*)

JONAS. They passed by.

STEPHEN. *(Yelling at them.)* Lucky bastards! That's right! Go that way! You would've been bloody hot sausage! *(Then, to* **JONAS**.*)* They're going toward the river and raising hell in that direction.

> *(**JONAS** puts down his stick. **STEPHEN** does not.)*

Hurry and pull those sheets off the garden. They'll ruin the cabbage. Hurry, Jonas. Pull them off.

JONAS. *(Still concerned about **Stephen**.)* That's the fourth stampede this month.

STEPHEN. It's the fifth. Each time they get closer. Damn Germans! I'm going to kill those pigs! The Common Council's probably behind this. Bastard Pigs!

JONAS. Never seen you this rageful. You're still holding your stick, Papa.

STEPHEN. *(Re: sheet with embroidered flowers.)* What is that you're holding, Jonas?

JONAS. What do you mean?

STEPHEN. What are you holding, boy? What is that?

JONAS. The sheet next to your bed.

STEPHEN. I told you to grab the sheets *off* my bed, not next to it.

JONAS. It's just a sheet, Papa.

STEPHEN. It was a sheet that was folded. Under my table and folded.

JONAS. I had just washed the others…

STEPHEN. It was folded and not to be bothered. I don't touch that sheet. It's never been touched. Why out of all these years you decide to touch it today?

JONAS. It's just a sheet, collecting dust.

STEPHEN. I don't care if it's collecting shit. It belonged to your mother!!!

(**JONAS** *is stunned. A pause.*)

It belonged to your mother. Her sheet, her embroider. It was hers.

JONAS. Papa... I didn't know.

STEPHEN. It's one of the few things I have left of her. And you have ruined it. Ruined! Give it to me! Give it to me, Jonas!

(*He snatches the sheet.*)

How could you be so absent-hearted! You continue to be absent-hearted! Too much drawing and park talk. Damn you, Jonas!

(**STEPHEN** *pushes him.*)

(**JONAS** *looks up at him, confused.*)

What?! What?!! (*Then, after a moment.*) Don't look at me like that.

JONAS. I didn't know... You never... It just sits under... I'll wash it for you.

STEPHEN. Come here, boy!!

(**JONAS** *goes to him.* **STEPHEN** *hugs him.*)

Forgive me. It was hers. Your mother's.

(*Looks at a confused* **JONAS**.)

I know I don't say it ever, but...you remind me of her. Alright?

JONAS. Is that good, Papa?

STEPHEN. Yes! Lots of thoughts in her head. Kind-hearted. A little stubborn. She liked stitching things on dresses and sheets. Sometimes I think she stitched herself right into this house. And she had a fancy for beer...

JONAS. I don't like beer.

STEPHEN. That's the only difference and it's a *shame*. *(Then.)* Come here.

    (**STEPHEN** *hugs him again.*)

JONAS. *(Manning up.)* I'll drink beer if you want.

STEPHEN. And force me to have to clean your puke? No thank you. *(Then.)* Your mother was a damn good woman, Jonas. I was with plenty before I married her and after. Most of them were the **ill-reputes** and I wasn't any different. I know you were a baby when those riots happened and somebody snatched her, but let me tell you: your mother's the only reason I'm still able to stand up in the world. She gave me strength. The way this world treat a man like me...makes you want to jump in the river and sink. I wasn't able to protect her and it's my life's biggest regret but I do hope I gave her something worth keeping. When you find a woman for yourself, make sure she helps you stand and you protect her for it. But you haven't found her yet. Understand?

JONAS. *(Confused but somehow knowing.)* Found who, Papa?

STEPHEN. You haven't found the woman you need in that **Paddy** girl. No matter what you believe.

JONAS. I'm fond of her, Papa. I'm more than fond of her. She *sees* me and I like to be seen.

STEPHEN. Like I said: You haven't found your woman yet! So... You stay *here* until you do. You and I are staying *here*! That's what your mother would want. And I'm thinking of building another story on the house soon and I'll need you for that. Alright?

(**JONAS** *says nothing.*)

STEPHEN. Alright?! Another story on the house! Me and you. Together.

JONAS. *(Awkward silence.)* Only if you come to my art lessons.

(The sound of pigs.)

STEPHEN. You hear that?! It's the pigs a-gain! They're coming back, Jonas.

JONAS. They always do, Papa.

STEPHEN. Yes. Always something out to undo what a man has done. Grab your stick! We're about to crack their bloody heads once and for all!

Scene Six

(Saturday. The Van Cleefs' front yard.)

*(**MARION** stands before **STEPHEN**, who holds a handful of money.)*

STEPHEN. There aren't a lot of people I like in the city anymore. They walk on your feet. Spit everywhere you step. Pick your pocket. Piss in alleys. And all that shit on the roads don't belong to just the hawses. But when thirty people walk up to *your* cart and buy you clean of oystahs, bloody fire! I like the people in New York. I will kiss the people in New York in the mouth. Today was a damn great day!

MARION. Stephen –

STEPHEN. *(Holds up money and rum.)* Thomas Downing can never say this happened to him. Not even on his good day, *with* his *salty* oystahs! I may have to build me another *house*! Get me some tenants!

MARION. Coppers came by Pete Richardson's last night.

STEPHEN. Is that why you're back in my face after I told you to stay away?

MARION. Yes, coppers roughed him up.

STEPHEN. Coppers are always roughing. Coppers rough! *(Holds money in both hands.)* I really can't believe this. How much do you think this is? You learned numbers at the African Free School. I'd say one hundred! How much?!

MARION. The coppers broke Pete's arm. Bruised him up. Phoebe is with he and his mother now.

STEPHEN. Bloody! Did I ask to hear about Pete?! *(Holds up money.)* I made more money today than I ever made and that's all that matters. *(Looking out.)* Even the wind is parting those trees for me. I can see the river and it looks rich. *(Grabs a bottle.)* I need to open up this rum.

MARION. Stephen! Pete went to the Council, questioned what they offered for his home. Coppers dragged him down by the Reservoir. Said if he came back, they'd break more than his arm.

STEPHEN. Well... Pete needs to learn how to fight back. Don't he? Over six feet tall and punch like a duck.

MARION. He's been a good neighbor. Births, deaths, he sits by your side with kindness. He's given you milk from his cow.

STEPHEN. He's tall as that maple and fights like he quacks. What are you doing here, Marion?

MARION. Pete and his mother are leaving later today. He's taking the Council's offer and moving to Weeksville. The rest of us are staying until we get our rightful monies.

STEPHEN. Sounds like you have a plan. Why do you need to tell me?

MARION. Stephen, we're marching down to the Council. Fifty names on the affidavit now. Folks have been asking for you to lead us.

STEPHEN. Lead? What the hell am I leading?

MARION. The folks in Seneca. To the Council.

STEPHEN. I need you to get out of my face before I show you these knuckles.

MARION. What happened to Pete is going to happen to others. Is that what you want? See one of your neighbors bludgeoned? These are good people here. You know how they do us.

STEPHEN. Yes – a Negro in this country is not allowed to speak up. They've got that written down. They'll kick you in the gut to remind you. And it's not New York I'm talking about. It's everywhere a Negro lives.

MARION. Stephen, you're not listening –

STEPHEN. I'm not leading anybody. Plenty of top-hat Negroes like Frederick Douglass walking around. Go bother him! *(Calling.)* Frederick Douglass, they need you!

MARION. We need *you* because of what you did in Five Points during those Riots.

STEPHEN. Oh hell and bloody fire! The Riots?!

MARION. You organized our people. Those Whites and Irish were ripping apart our homes, beating us. Because they believed the abolitionists were teaching Jesus was black. Remember?

STEPHEN. Yes – I remember that I was a fool.

MARION. Your name still means something, Stephen. If the Council sees you marching us down there – they might buckle.

STEPHEN. What about your name? You made deals during the Riots. Told folks the city would protect us if we cut ties with that church. Think I forgot? That's probably what you trying to do now. Sell Seneca out.

MARION. I was young and I really thought cutting ties would help.

STEPHEN. But it didn't and they still stuffed money in your pockets. Let you start that little shoe trade.

MARION. I also used that money to get fugitives to Ontario, Nova Scotia. I'm still doing it.

STEPHEN. Negroes can't afford to make mistakes! Not then. Not now.

MARION. Forget about me. I know it's hard – losing Susie in those Riots.

STEPHEN. *(Taken aback.)* What?

MARION. Susie –

STEPHEN. *(Stepping toward* **MARION**.*)* Say her name a-gain. See what happens to you.

MARION. She was proud of you that day at the Riots. You still got that fire in you.

STEPHEN. *(Absolute.)* That day took more than it gave. You wouldn't know anything about that.

MARION. I know they're building a park, forcing us to leave, threatening our lives. That I do know and you do too. But I can't rally people alone. I need you for this. Friend to friend.

STEPHEN. We haven't been friends in a long time. I just tolerate you for my son.

MARION. Then...I reckon God will be our only defense.

STEPHEN. Reckon he'll have to be. Because today is the best day of my life!

> (**MARION** *leaves as* **STEPHEN** *takes a few steps forward. He sees something through the trees.)*

STEPHEN. Look at that! A whale! Keep swimming, you beast. Today – we're both rich.

Scene Seven

(A bit later. Cemetery.)

*(***JONAS*** *sits.* ***BRIDGET*** *enters.)*

BRIDGET. I looked for ye earlier. Thought ye forgot about me.

JONAS. I was at my art lesson. Then left for the hotel. Worked a short shift.

BRIDGET. Brought you more oatcake if you want it. Me ma had extra. She sweetened it with molasses this time. A dandy on Bloomingdale was handing out free buckets.

(She hands him a cake but he doesn't eat it.)

Is your tongue sleeping? Thought you liked the cakes.

JONAS. I do.

(He nibbles on cake.)

BRIDGET. Can we just sit. Hold hands for a while. In the quiet. No work for me today.

JONAS. If that's what you prefer.

(She sits next to him.)

(Silence. Then:)

BRIDGET. Never known you to be this somber. What's the matter with ye? Didn't ye lesson go well?

JONAS. We could invite guests today. I placed a chair in front for Papa with the other guests. But he never showed. I waited outside, even after everyone left for Pfaff's. I thought he'd show up. To see what I do, just for once. He didn't show.

*(***BRIDGET*** *holds his hand. Then:)*

BRIDGET. Perhaps our da's won't ever be who we dream them to be.

JONAS. Perhaps.

>*(Beat)*

>*(Noticing another small bruise on her face.)* Did yours hit your mouth?

BRIDGET. What?

JONAS. Your mouth's bruised again.

BRIDGET. He was… throwing things. I moved too slowly. I'm such the tortoise.

JONAS. Bridget, he hit you. I know he did.

BRIDGET. *(Looks at gravestone.)* You know what they believe in Galway?

>*(**JONAS** says nothing.)*

Do you know, Jonas?

JONAS. *(Going along.)* Dragons fly and blow fires?

BRIDGET. Yes and you tease about it, but it's true…

JONAS. What do they say in Galway?

BRIDGET. They say the dead don't rest 'til another takes their place, takes on the burden they couldn't finish.

JONAS. *(Confused.)* I don't understand what that means.

BRIDGET. Maybe it's the same for the living, Jonas. You and me – we're just as tired, waiting for someone or something to take our burdens.

JONAS. Maybe we don't have a choice.

>*(A rustle behind startles them.)*

BRIDGET. Somebody's watching us.

JONAS. There's nobody there but the dead A.M.E. Zion.

BRIDGET. Can we just sit and be quiet?

JONAS. Yes. The quiet is the best thing the day has to offer.

(After a moment...)

BRIDGET. Jonas – I have something more to say.

JONAS. What?

BRIDGET. Dragons in Galway do fly and they breathe fire.

(They both laugh as they hold each other's hands.)

Scene Eight

(The Van Cleef house.)

(Midnight.)

(**STEPHEN** – *drinking rum – stands in front of the house. Singing:*)

STEPHEN.

DRINK TO ME ONLY WITH THINE EYES
AND I WILL PLEDGE WITH MINE.
OR LEAVE A KISS WITHIN THE CUP...

(He picks through a barrel of freshly-caught oysters. An owl hoots. He hoots back at it. The owl hoots again. He hoots back.)

(Then an explosion nearby. The house rattles. Thousands of red embers fall from the sky like rain.)

(**STEPHEN** *stiffens. For a moment, he says nothing. Then, looking up and clutching his oyster cart –)*

Damn your explosions! You'll have to bury me on this land before I let it go.

End of Act One

ACT TWO

Scene One

(The Van Cleef house.)

(STEPHEN *stands on his ladder, making progress on the roof.* **PHOEBE** *stands at the yard.)*

PHOEBE. Stephen, the Parkers never went to the Council or signed anything. But they were still attacked. Red-faced coppers, entertained by the wreckage. Like that dynamite was planned.

STEPHEN. I've known New York coppers plan and do worse than that. So does everyone up here. Nothing new to report as far as I see.

PHOEBE. Those embers were flying through Seneca – could have sent this whole place on fire. You're telling me that didn't rile your nerves?

STEPHEN. I thought it was a fireworks show. Like that one in London. Bonfire Night. Had me a good time.

(STEPHEN continues working on the roof.)

PHOEBE. Well, this one killed the Parkers' chickens. A goat too.

STEPHEN. I'm about to throw this tin. Move unless you want a gash.

PHOEBE. You're up there patching roofs while they tear ours down?

STEPHEN. Yes – because it's my money, my roof, my life. And you're disturbing it.

PHOEBE. *(New tone, more personal.)* You're still who I look up to. And up there, you're telling me Seneca's already lost.

STEPHEN. Jesus wept! You and Marion are some hard-headed Negroes... Move, Phoebe! *(Holding tin.)*

PHOEBE. Your threats won't stop me, Stephen.

STEPHEN. *(Pauses, then with bitterness.)* You think I forgot what this city does to Negroes who stand in its way? Five Points, Seneca. It's all the same firing squad. I lost Susie fighting once to that hawse shit. I won't be the one standing in front this time. Alright?

PHOEBE. Mister Parker heard one of the coppers mention your name.

(**STEPHEN** *pauses.*)

STEPHEN. What they mention me for? Somebody got a fancy for my name? It's taken.

PHOEBE. He said they're coming for you.

STEPHEN. What depths you're going to travel with this pageantry, woman? Go teach a child to read.

PHOEBE. I'm telling the truth. They know what you're capable of.

STEPHEN. Well, let them come. I have ten fingers and the memory of how to use them.

PHOEBE. Why not use them now? Use them to help me?

STEPHEN. First you want me to sign papers. Now you want me to die swinging fists. Make up your mind.

PHOEBE. My mind is made. I want to arm myself.

STEPHEN. Like Toussaint of your great Haiti.

PHOEBE. Yes.

STEPHEN. From where I'm stand – looks like you have enough war in you to fight two nations.

PHOEBE. They used dynamite, Stephen. What next? Cannons?

STEPHEN. How do I know Marion didn't light that fuse himself? He's got it in him.

PHOEBE. Stephen, stop all of this... It's childish.

STEPHEN. Look, I have fought enough battles for other people to know how it ends. I'm put in front and my knuckles get broke. My life. And you all go on living. That won't happen again. *(Returns to ladder.)* Y'all need to prepare yourselves for your own battle. Drop dynamite on them. Be Toussaint.

MARION. *(Entering.)* Phoebe! What are you doing? Somebody's started a fire at William Pease's grocery. We need to get over there.

PHOEBE. That's fine. Because he's a lost cause.

MARION. He's not a lost cause. He's just scared. Let him enjoy his little money and let's go.

STEPHEN. Scared? Only thing that scares me is sleeping in the streets.

MARION. *(Sarcastic.)* Well, you have enough money now. So that won't happen. Let's go, Phoebe.

PHOEBE. *(To* **STEPHEN**.*)* After Epiphany Davis, the A.M.E. Zion Church used every wage they had so we can own property – this is your stance?

STEPHEN. Why are you dragging up those dead Negroes? They didn't build this place for me.

PHOEBE. Them owning property allowed them to vote so they can have a say about our lives in this city. They did build Seneca for you...and you want to stand like that's not worth puke.

MARION. – Phoebe, come on, William Pease needs us – let this man enjoy his riches -

STEPHEN. Let me tell you: If those Riots hadn't happened, I'd be in Five Points. I wouldn't be here.

PHOEBE. Five Points?

STEPHEN. Yes! Heard of it?! Where every Negro you know comes from. You've got shame for it now?

PHOEBE. You'd rather go back there? Drinking, dancing the Juba, fathering bastards?

STEPHEN. Yes – those folks looked out for me. They didn't have notion to sacrifice my life so theirs could be better.

MARION. *(Disgusted by what was said.)* Dear God – we've damn-near slit our wrists for you and Jonas. Stripped the clothes off our backs.

> *(Angry, crossing to **STEPHEN**.)*

Where is the gratitude? Where is the thanks?

PHOEBE. *(To **MARION**.)* He has none. He rather have his son drunk like those folks in Five Points.

STEPHEN. I want Jonas to know what brotherhood looks like. Not following behind a bunch of fancy petticoats and dandy suits.

MARION. *(Angry.)* I'll be over to William Pease's.

> *(He exits.)*

PHOEBE. Since you care so much about Jonas, stand up for him. For Susie. She would want you to. She wanted to live here. With you. Because she saw something in you then.

> *(**STEPHEN** crosses to Susie's embroidered sheet and – impulsively rips it.)*

STEPHEN. Well, she's not here now is she?

PHOEBE. Ou kraze kè m *(Translation: You break my heart.)*

STEPHEN. Will you leave now? William Pease needs you.

PHOEBE. *(Softening tone.)* Your son is watching every move you don't make.

STEPHEN. Good. Let him learn how a man lives.

> (**PHOEBE** *exits.*)

I don't fight anyone's battles anymore! Get your own dynamite.

> (**STEPHEN** *stands there. Alone. He looks at the ripped sheet and immediately feels regret but he pushes on. He lifts the new tin sheet, hammer in hand – and begins nailing it to the roof. One hollow blow.)*

Scene Two

(Sunday.)

(Front of Van Cleef house.)

*(**STEPHEN** is on a ladder, making more progress with the roof as he sings:)*

STEPHEN.
I SENT THEE LATE A ROSY WREATH, NOT SO MUCH HON'RING THEE
AS GIVING IT A HOPE THAT THERE IT COULD NOT WITHERED BE...

*(**MATHIUS** enters.)*

MATHIUS. Guten Tag, Mister Van Cleef. Same song as before. Your voice improves.

STEPHEN. *(Unapologetic and stepping down.)* I'm not here to impress you, Mathius. But it's a song my wife used to sing, if you need to know.

(He walks to a pot of coffee.)

What is it that you want?

MATHIUS. *(Evading.)* How long has it been since she dead?

STEPHEN. She's not dead. Who told you that? Who told you my wife was dead?!

MATHIUS. But you're a widow, no? A Witwer? This is what they say.

STEPHEN. What are you doing here a-gain, Mathius?

MATHIUS. My hand is better now because of you.

STEPHEN. So them coppers are over you living among Negroes?

MATHIUS. I'm told they jostle many of the new ones. Not to fret.

STEPHEN. *(Noticing* **MATHIUS**' *nervousness.)* Then why is your hands shaking? Something's got you bothered?

MATHIUS. No. It is nothing.

(Changing topics.) My cough stopped, Mister Van Cleef.

STEPHEN. Your cough?

MATHIUS. Yes. I wrote last night to my family in Württemberg. Told them of your concern. I told them your concern stopped the cough. And you're like a father to me.

STEPHEN. That's what you wrote them? I'm like a father? You ponder me that deeply, Mathius?

MATHIUS. Yes. Dankbarkeit. Your generosity is cherished.

STEPHEN. Who you think you joshing, boy? What's going on here?

MATHIUS. It is true what I feel for you. I want you to know this.

STEPHEN. What's going on here, Mathius? I need you to be a man right now and speak the truth.

MATHIUS. But you like me, don't you, Mister Van Cleef? You have concern. About my cough, where I live and work. I write my family this. I have kind heart, Mister Van Cleef.

STEPHEN. I asked you to be a man! Stick out your gut, what do you want?

MATHIUS. ...They're making plans to come here. The municipal police. The coppers.

STEPHEN. So you're now their bloody messenger?

MATHIUS. Mayor Wood says we may have to use force on "Nigger Village."

STEPHEN. Nigger Village, huh? That's what he said? The mayor?

MATHIUS. You all are not behave. Most of Irish leaving. I move few days ago.

STEPHEN. Did you? *(Then.)* Most of the Irish or *you* don't own anything. *I* own.

MATHIUS. The park must be built. The city always changing. I mention this to you. The mayor and Common Council has their orders and we must follow...

STEPHEN. We or *you*?

MATHIUS. They say you refuse monies, for your home. Why is this?

STEPHEN. *(Surprised he knows this.)* You seem to know so much; why don't you tell me?

MATHIUS. They offer good value, they say. And you say no. This is not good way to do.

STEPHEN. Is that why they're using explosives? *(An epiphany.)* Or was it you, Mathius? Up here bruising up folks, nearly catching Seneca on fire?

MATHIUS. Don't ask me this, Mister Van Cleef.

STEPHEN. You show up here shaking like a wet dog, can't look me in the eye – are you behind all of this mayhem?

MATHIUS. They make me help. It's not my will.

STEPHEN. Don't you dare bring your cowardice to my door. You want to serve them, serve them. But don't pretend like it ain't your hands that's bloody.

MATHIUS. You misunderstand, Mister Van Cleef.

STEPHEN. Well...I've survived plenty in this City. I'm from six generations of survivors in this City. If you look at me hard, you'll see all six generations in my face and in these fists. A few coppers may scare Pete Richardson or the Parkers, but not me.

MATHIUS. They're going to tear it down soon.

STEPHEN. *(Showing some concern.)* Tear it down how? What's that mean?

MATHIUS. I can't say but I'm here because I care, Mister Van Cleef.

STEPHEN. What do you want? A stuffed goose for Thanksgiving?! Huh?

MATHIUS. Mister Van Cleef, I did not come to this country to do this!!! To be this person! Ein Verräter. *(Translation: A traitor.)* It was not the wish of my family. They think I'm here respectful. But it's not what I thought, Mister Van Cleef. They make me this... I don't know what to do. I don't want this.

STEPHEN. Nothing is what you want it to be in this city. It just shows up in your face and you either face it or take to your heels.

MATHIUS. I don't want harm for anyone.

*(**STEPHEN** retreats to the ladder and climbs.)*

Bitte, Mister Van Cleef. They need to accept the offer.

STEPHEN. *(Emotionally exhausted.)* I'm done with you for the day, Mathius.

MATHIUS. They say you have until nightfall.

STEPHEN. Have some oystahs before you go. Fried them with garlic and curry. Real tasty on the tongue. Surprised even me. Grab some from that pan. You can take some back to your respectful thugs. Tell them it's a gift from one Negro who's not scared of anything. And stop calling me, Mister Van Cleef. I don't want your formalities!

Scene Three

(Seneca Village.)

(Late night Sunday.)

*(**MATHIUS** stands on a hill.)*

(He holds a megaphone to his mouth.)

(Using his best English.)

MATHIUS. This is New York City Municipal Police. On behalf of Mayor Fernando Wood, we advise if you do not vacate Seneca by sunrise, we will be force to move you ourselves. Please take all of your belongings and goods or they will be destroyed. Men, women, children, be advised, if you stay we will move you. *(Slight break in voice.)* This was your home...I...know this. But... *(Returns to original tone.)* Eminent domain is now. You are trespassing. You are trespassers on this land. We don't want harm for you, but know we will use force. You have until sunrise. This is New York City Municipal Police! On behalf of Mayor Fernando Wood!

Scene Four

(Later. Midnight.)

(Cemetery.)

*(**JONAS** stands and draws as **PHOEBE** approaches, with something on her mind.)*

PHOEBE. Be careful out here. Didn't you hear the coppers? The threat?

JONAS. I did. Yes.

PHOEBE. Do you need any vinegar? I have some. These mosquitoes will leave marks on you like a whip. Especially this time of night.

JONAS. I'm fine. A few bites don't fret me. What brings you *here*?

PHOEBE. A woman can't wander on her own in your opinion?

JONAS. No, I mean – You never come here.

PHOEBE. I used to. Years ago. Read; sing hymns. *(Not singing; remembering a hymn.)* "Dark was the night, and cold the ground, On which the Lord was laid."

JONAS. I was working, Mrs. Phoebe. Not much time to myself –

PHOEBE. *(Glancing at his drawing)* Bodies again? Thighs?

JONAS. No bodies today. This is…something else.

PHOEBE. *(Distracted.)* You feel that? I do love the breeze as it blows through those sycamores.

JONAS. I was really needing to finish this –

PHOEBE. *(Brief pause, then changing subject.)* My cousin Olga traveled to Paris a while back.

JONAS. *(Curious.)* Your cousin went to Paris?

PHOEBE. Yes. Morally, there was a lot to question. All that wine drinking. And debauchery. But she did enjoy their parks. The Jardin des Tuileries was her favorite. She said there were lots of elm trees. Hundreds. Statues of painters; queens. Art! The day she was there, she stumbled upon a large group of people, sitting on blankets, listening to a man on violin. The sweetest moment she ever had, she said. Tres magnifique. I reckon that's what they'll do here. Where we're standing. Lie on the grass and listen to men on violins.

JONAS. I reckon they will.

PHOEBE. My baby is buried out here.

JONAS. Your baby? You had a baby, Mrs. Phoebe?

PHOEBE. A boy. Would have been your age. He lived long enough to grow two bottom teeth. But not long enough for me to name him. He lays under those Sycamores.

JONAS. I'm sorry. I'm so sorry. I didn't know.

PHOEBE. Dead babies don't survive public memory. Like *some* people don't. *(Begins to weep.)*

JONAS. Do you want to sit down? I don't have anything for you to rest upon –

PHOEBE. They're going to take all of this from us, Jonas. Like we never existed. *Mattered. (Then.)* Where are you going to go? What's your plan?

JONAS. Papa believes if he stays, they won't build the park.

PHOEBE. And what do *you* think? You heard the threat. What they're eager to do to us.

JONAS. I don't want to think, mam.

PHOEBE. But now is the time to put your foot forward. If you want art, you should chase after it. Or whatever lights a fire in you. Do you hear me?

JONAS. Yes, mam –

PHOEBE. That threat has Marion fevered with rage. He's going to the Common Council in the morning. Alone. To demand full value on behalf of everyone here. A lunatic's notion for certain.

JONAS. He shouldn't go. Beg him not to. The Council is filth.

PHOEBE. You know what they wrote about us today in the *Daily Tribune*? They called us bloodsuckers. Insects. Simple-minded. I taught as many as I could here in Seneca. There's nothing simple-minded about any of us. They tell themselves whatever they need to justify what they do to us. Justify their corruption.

JONAS. *(To himself.)* They called us insects?

PHOEBE. A part of me wants to burn up this entire place so they can't build anything. *Everywhere we go, everything we try to have...* They're going to build this park, Jonas, and we won't be permitted to frolic in it. Put our feet in the grass.

JONAS. Pardon my papa, Mrs. Phoebe. I wish he were a different kind of man...

PHOEBE. If you were our son – I know that's selfish to say, but –

JONAS. I'll go with Marion. To the council.

PHOEBE. What? No. You stay here. Let Marion be the foolish warrior.

JONAS. I'm going with him. Seneca is my home too.

PHOEBE. Oh, Jonas.

> *(Hugs **JONAS**. Then breaks away.)*

There it is a-gain. That breeze.

JONAS. *(Re: breeze.)* I feel it.

PHOEBE. It reminds me... even when the world is ugly there's something gentle here.

Scene Five

(The cemetery.)

(Morning.)

(**BRIDGET** *holds something inside a cloth.* **JONAS** *is a bit preoccupied.)*

BRIDGET. Are ye eyes closed?

JONAS. Yes, yes.

BRIDGET. Both of 'em.

JONAS. They're both closed.

BRIDGET. Stick out yer hand.

(**JONAS** *does so. She puts a large watch in his hand.)*

Open yer eyes.

JONAS. A watch? Did you spend all of your wages on this?

BRIDGET. I left my lady this morning. Told her I couldn't clean any more of her chamberpots. Tired of her stink on me hands.

JONAS. And she offered you a watch?

BRIDGET. She said if I left, she wouldn't pay me. Said she'd throw one of her cats on me head. She said that, I tell ya.

JONAS. So how did you get the watch?

BRIDGET. Do you like it?

JONAS. It's grand. Real dandy. A rich man's watch.

BRIDGET. I took it from me lady because she owed me. It was in her parlor and I grabbed it off the table. *(Then.)* Why are ye eyeing me? Thought you liked it.

JONAS. She's going to look for it. She'll come after you. Someone tarred and feathered an Irish girl on Reade Street for stealing eggs.

BRIDGET. Well, she won't step foot up here looking, will she. And if she does, I'll tell everyone she bathes with her cats. Because she does. All four of 'em. They'll suckle her teat if she lets them.

JONAS. Bridget, she's going to come after you...

BRIDGET. Lets sit down. In the quiet. I need quiet. No noise.

(They sit.)

JONAS. You can't keep the watch. It's not yours.

BRIDGET. Whose is it then?

JONAS. It's your lady's. It belongs to her. You can't steal from your employers.

BRIDGET. She can have me cleaning her slop, boiling her dirty sheets, call me a "pot licker" in front of her lady friends. Me family is poor off but we never licked the bottom of pots. I've earned this. It's mine.

JONAS. Bridget, I want to speak with you.

BRIDGET. Could you keep the watch for me? If my father finds it he'll try to sell it. I don't want money for it. It's me badge of honor.

JONAS. I'll bury it out here.

(He digs a small hole and buries it.)

Done.

BRIDGET. Come sit with me. Let's close our eyes.

JONAS. I have something to do later...

BRIDGET. What?

JONAS. I'm certain you heard the police, the threat?

(**BRIDGET** *shrugs. She doesn't want to talk about it.*)

JONAS. At my lesson on Saturday, my teacher asks if I considered her paying my passage to Paris.

BRIDGET. Why? Thought you weren't going there.

JONAS. I think we should go. Live decent for a year or so. (*Silence from her.*) Bridget?

BRIDGET. What do you mean?

JONAS. Or we can move downtown. Or anywhere. We can't stay here.

BRIDGET. Why do ye say "we"?

JONAS. You and I should go together.

BRIDGET. Oh.

JONAS. Any thought on the matter?

BRIDGET. Can we be quiet? Close our eyes? Listen to the crickets.

JONAS. We should go somewhere, Bridget. What do you think?

BRIDGET. Why should we go?

JONAS. Because...we... Things are changing. Coppers might harm us if we don't leave.

BRIDGET. I like to be quiet.

JONAS. No! I will not be quiet. I don't feel like being quiet. No!

BRIDGET. What's the matter with ye?

JONAS. I know your father is putting bruises on you.

(**BRIDGET** *flinches away from him.*)

Every time I see you it's a new one. There's even one now on your wrist. Now you're stealing watches. You say you don't like this city, well, I don't like what it's doing to you. We need to get out of here, Bridget. Go to Paris, anywhere.

BRIDGET. I don't like your tone.

JONAS. I don't care if you don't like it. It's what you're going to get.

BRIDGET. I need you to speak to me differently.

JONAS. We can't pretend Seneca isn't in danger, Bridget.

BRIDGET. I'm not pretending.

JONAS. Yes you are. Those coppers want to hurt us. They want to destroy our homes.

BRIDGET. I don't need to hear this. I just want to sit and have a little peace for a moment.

JONAS. All you do is pretend, Bridget. You pretend the park isn't coming, you pretend your papa isn't a brute. You want to sit here with me among the dead and pretend the world out there isn't an ugly place.

BRIDGET. While we're here it isn't.

JONAS. It's not real, Bridget.

BRIDGET. Neither is painting pictures.

*(Off **JONAS**' hurt look.)* I didn't mean that. Just stay with me and let's make it all real.

JONAS. *(Deep breath.)* Leave with me or…leave me alone!

*(Silence. Frustrated, **BRIDGET** exits.)*

(Another silence. Then…)

*(**JONAS** notices one of the headstones is vandalized with the words "Nigger Village.")*

(As lights fade, we fade up on the sound of a violent confrontation between many people.)

Scene Six

(The Van Cleefs' house.)

(Later that day.)

(**STEPHEN** *stands with his fighting stick. In defense mode.*)

STEPHEN. *(Concerned and calling out.)* Jonas! Jonas! Jonas!

PHOEBE. *(From offstage, frantic.)* Stephen!

(**STEPHEN** *steps forward as* **PHOEBE** *enters with an injured* **MARION.**)

STEPHEN. Is Jonas with you?

(Noticing **MARION** *has a bruised face, arm.)*

What happened to him?

PHOEBE. Somebody grabbed him from behind. Held both of his arms, so he couldn't move. Then another one stepped in front of him.

STEPHEN. Coppers, then. It's always how they send their message.

(**STEPHEN** *puts down his stick.*)

MARION. They clubbed me good. Thought I lost my eye.

PHOEBE. They wanted to kill him. Leave him for dead. Rats picking at him.

STEPHEN. Did you recognize anyone then? Coppers aren't hard to see.

MARION. No. They came from behind me –

PHOEBE. Je pourrais les tuer. *(Translation: I could kill them.)*

(**STEPHEN** *crosses to grab some salve for* **MARION**'s *wounds.*)

STEPHEN. Here. Put this on his face.

MARION. They *did* say if we didn't leave by tonight, they'd hurt Phoebe.

STEPHEN. Hurt? What way did they say it? Who said that?

MARION. You know the way, Stephen. She's a woman. What way do you think? They did this to get to you.

STEPHEN. They want me, they know how to find me.

MARION. Well, they found me instead. The council laughed in my face when I demanded people's proper value. Then offered me seven hundred dollars. We're going to take it and leave for Philadelphia this evening.

STEPHEN. Philadelphia?

PHOEBE. What?

MARION. This evening. There's a **Colored** coach before sunset.

PHOEBE. Now you make decisions without me?

MARION. They're going to build this park. And no matter what we say or do, we're in their way. I'm not willing to risk your life for this.

STEPHEN. Running to Philadelphia sounds like a coward's move.

MARION. It's not about saving. It's about protecting. They'll tear this place apart and no one will lift a finger to help us.

PHOEBE. Marion, we've worked too hard for our home to let them do this to us. Seneca is our peace.

MARION. Our peace left as soon as they decided to build this park.

PHOEBE. I want to fight, Marion. In Haiti, the people wouldn't let –

MARION. Well, we don't have the numbers they had in Haiti. Mayor Wood doesn't want us here! He don't care about our education, or that we own property. They laugh at that or rip it to pieces. Stephen, I need you and Jonas to come with us. To Philadelphia.

STEPHEN. What?! I'm not leaving anywhere. Nor is my son. I need to go and find him.

(**PHOEBE** *and* **MARION** *exchange a glance.*)

PHOEBE. Isn't he here?

STEPHEN. Why would he be here? You heard me calling for him when you showed up.

MARION. Earlier...he said he might meet me down by the Council but he didn't show.

STEPHEN. Then where the bloody damn is he?

PHOEBE. We don't know, Stephen.

STEPHEN. You all don't know where my son is? (*Calling out.*) Jonas!

MARION. We're not keeping anything from you. We just weren't sure.

STEPHEN. (*Brief silence.*) You lost him, just like you lost Susie.

MARION. What the hell are you talking about?

STEPHEN. You heard me. You lost her.

MARION. We helped you look for her, Stephen. In Brooklyn, Staten Island –

PHOEBE. You were the one who gave up. Disappeared into a bottle of rum.

STEPHEN. No, I looked for her. For twenty-one days. No sleep, nothing.

MARION. You looked until it got too hard. Then you drank. We stepped in. Helped out with Jonas when you couldn't.

PHOEBE. If you don't know where Jonas is – it's because of you, not us.

MARION. That's your truth, man. Start living with it. We do.

STEPHEN. *(Feeling the sting of truth.)* Go to bloody hell.

MARION. You can't fight this city alone, Stephen. Now we're leaving tonight. Before sunset.

> *(**STEPHEN** looks at them both. Not contemplating their offer, but holding back his growing rage.)*

STEPHEN. Go! But if anything's happened to my son I –

> *(He wants to blame them but he knows he can't. He snatches up his stick and exits fast, calling into the night.)*

Jonas!

Scene Seven

(The Van Cleefs' front yard.)

(A bit later.)

*(**JONAS** sits. Quiet, contemplative. His face, bruised.)*

*(**STEPHEN** walks up, without showing emotion.)*

STEPHEN. I was out looking for you. For a good while.

JONAS. I'm fine.

STEPHEN. You don't look fine... Where have you been?

JONAS. I went down to the Common Council. Got into a tussle with a man who wouldn't let me in.

STEPHEN. You did what?! *(Catching himself.)* Let me fry up some oystahs. Looks like you're hungry. Like you haven't eaten for days. Months.

(He goes to the oyster cart.)

JONAS. They're leaving, aren't they? Marion and Mrs. Phoebe?

STEPHEN. They're doing what they need to do. We're not them. We do what *we* need to do. Are you certain you're alright? I didn't know if someone had hurt...

JONAS. *(Unwavered.)* Where are they going?

STEPHEN. I don't know. Somewhere cowards go I reckon.

JONAS. When are they leaving?

STEPHEN. Is that the family you want? Gamble your life for them? Fret over their whereabouts? You had no cause to go down there to that Council.

JONAS. Somebody had to.

(A beat, then:)

STEPHEN. No one has do nothing. If you don't want any oystahs, just say so. No reason to labor if I don't have to.

JONAS. I want to go to Paris. Or live downtown. And draw.

STEPHEN. I really think we should just eat these on the half shell. It'll take too long to heat up the oil.

JONAS. Did you hear me?

STEPHEN. You're not going anywhere. Especially if it's about you becoming a dandy downtown. Drawing pictures. I won't let you. And Paris? No!

JONAS. You won't let me? I work at a hotel. I make my own wages.

STEPHEN. Barely enough to keep the drawers on your legs. You're not going anywhere.

JONAS. My drawing teacher says I got talent and she'll give me money to leave here.

STEPHEN. She what? You don't take charity from anybody.

JONAS. It's not charity. She likes my drawings.

STEPHEN. You trying to run off with the poor Paddy girl? Is that what you're brewing? You can't take care of yourself. Look at your face. How are you going to take care of that Paddy girl? How can you do anything for yourself?

JONAS. Her name is Bridget. Don't call her a Paddy girl.

STEPHEN. You just count your lucky stars I let you creep around here with her. Bet you don't even know you have to scrub your privates good after being with women. *(Slight pause.)* Do you want something to eat or not?

JONAS. I know how to wash myself, Papa.

STEPHEN. I beg to differ.

JONAS. You don't even know what I draw. You don't even look at it.

STEPHEN. What you want me to look at? Some pictures? I see you drawing a whole lot but I never see you drawing me. Why should I care what you draw?

JONAS. You know, I stay here because I don't think you can live on *your* own.

STEPHEN. What did you say to me? Stand up straight and say that a-gain.

JONAS. *(Bolder.)* I stay here because you can't live on your own.

STEPHEN. Bloody! I have been on my own since I was twelve years old. After both of my parents died of cholera cause the water in the city was full of hawse and pig shit and everything else. I had to leave school and turn to those streets and do whatever I could to live. I found oystahs and they saved my life. I will always be able to live on my own. I don't need anybody's help.

(He grabs some rum and takes a swallow.)

JONAS. Are you going to drink yourself to sleep?

STEPHEN. Say that once more?

JONAS. Is that why my mother never returned? She didn't like you anymore?

STEPHEN. Somebody has stepped into their boots and feel like they're fitting.

JONAS. Sometimes I watch you sleep to make certain you wake up. I get up every day and boil your clothes, because if I didn't, you wouldn't. I wash the floors. I wash the windows. All you do is go out everyday and sell and cook oystahs. Then you come home and go right back to that river. I stay around in case you slow down and realize you're alone and you may need me.

STEPHEN. I don't need anybody.

JONAS. That's not true.

STEPHEN. This city forces you not to count on anybody. You can't count on anybody.

JONAS. You need me.

STEPHEN. All I need is for nobody to steal you. Because they'll do it. They'll see you drawing something, walking alone, anything. They'll find a way.

JONAS. That doesn't happen every day. I have my wits. I'm strong.

STEPHEN. So was your mother. And I don't want to hear anything else on it.

JONAS. That's not going to happen to me.

STEPHEN. Nobody knows what's going to happen. Life is a gamble and will always try to knock you down.

JONAS. We have to leave, Papa. The city and the Mayor are forcing us to leave.

Pushing your chest out isn't going to change that. We should collect the monies they're offering.

STEPHEN. We don't have to do anything, but stay where we belong.

JONAS. We can't stay here. I can't stay. What is wrong with you?

STEPHEN. I'm a fighter. That's what's wrong. I'm a fighter! What is wrong with *you*?!

JONAS. But you haven't fought! You have not fought!!

(A very brief silence.)

STEPHEN. You're staying right here with me, Jonas. Understand? No Paris, no downtown, no Bridget, nothing.

JONAS. *(Absolute.)* I am leaving, Papa.

STEPHEN. *(Doubling down.)* If you leave, you better never show your face a-gain.

JONAS. You don't mean half of what you say.

(Slight beat.)

STEPHEN. Then you certainly don't know your father. Because I mean *everything* I say.

Scene Eight

(Lights up on **JONAS** *and* **BRIDGET**. **JONAS** *is bruised up a bit.)*

(A bit later. Cemetery.)

BRIDGET. I'm going with ye.

JONAS. Do you mean to Paris?

BRIDGET. Wherever. You do want me to go with ye?

JONAS. I do want you to go. I do. You're going with me, Bridget?

BRIDGET. Me family's moved out of the shanty. So I'm going with ye.

JONAS. Yes you are. Yes.

(He hugs her.)

BRIDGET. *(Re: his face, worried.)* I see you've been doing some things.

JONAS. I didn't have any other choice.

BRIDGET. I just wanted to let ye know I was going. So ye can prepare yerself.

JONAS. I don't need any preparation for you, Bridget.

(A beat.)

BRIDGET. When we travel, we'll eat together? Right?

JONAS. We will.

BRIDGET. And sleep in the same bed?

JONAS. Yes. If that's what you favor? Cause I'll favor it. *(Then.)* Pardon me for the last time I saw you –

BRIDGET. *(Interrupting.)* And if we go to Paris, can we also go to Galway?

JONAS. Yes. Yes. Anywhere. Everywhere.

BRIDGET. I just want to stop by and say hello to me grandmother.

JONAS. We can do that.

> (**BRIDGET** *pauses, doesn't move.*)

What is it? Say it.

BRIDGET. Lets stand here in the quiet and say goodbye to Seneca.

> (*She pulls him to her. They close their eyes.*)

Goodbye, smelly swamp.

JONAS. It's not so bad.

BRIDGET. Yes, it is. It's awful.

JONAS. Goodbye, reservoir.

BRIDGET. Goodbye dead people.

JONAS. Goodbye, pigs! You've made our lives hell!

BRIDGET. I reckon Seneca's not so bad.

JONAS. No. It's not.

BRIDGET. (*Shifting tone.*) I want to thank ye, Jonas.

JONAS. For what?

BRIDGET. For giving me something to ponder other than me poor circumstance.

JONAS. I...

BRIDGET. And I hope I brought something to ye.

JONAS. You brought... You *bring* me friendship. Happiness.

BRIDGET. I want to kiss you, right now, on the mouth.

JONAS. Out here, among the dead?

BRIDGET. Yes.

>   *(She kisses him, then:)*

I can't go with you.

JONAS. What? Why not?

BRIDGET. I want to but –

JONAS. You just said – a moment ago –

BRIDGET. I thought seeing ye would help me go. But… I have to stay and help me ma. Go where she goes. I really do. I can't leave her with me da'.

JONAS. She can go with us. I can find more wages. Please.

BRIDGET. You're gonna need to bring sunshine to someone else's sad eyes.

JONAS. I don't want to go anywhere without you. You see me, Bridget. You see me.

BRIDGET. I'm sorry, Jonas. You're an angel. God sent ye.

JONAS. No. Think about it a-gain. Your mind is blurry. Clear up your mind.

BRIDGET. I can't leave me ma with him. He's not you.

>   *(She exits.)*

Scene Nine

(The Van Cleefs'. Morning.)

(Lights up on **STEPHEN**. *Eating oysters and eyeing* **JONAS** *as he places a few items – matches, vegetables – into a traveling bag.)*

STEPHEN. Don't you need a hat? If you're traveling that far, you may want to wear a hat.

JONAS. Not sure how far I'm traveling.

STEPHEN. Well, you are traveling, aren't you? Looks to me like you're going somewhere.

JONAS. Yes.

STEPHEN. Wherever you go it's certainly... *(Then.) And* you still need a hat.

JONAS. I just needed to collect a few things –

STEPHEN. I'm saying you leaving here to be a dandy downtown or Paris, or wherever. You're gonna need a hat. All those dandy Negroes wear hats.

JONAS. I don't have a hat.

*(***STEPHEN*** hands ***JONAS*** a box.)*

STEPHEN. Here. Bought it from a milliner down on Park Place. One of the best in the city. He wasn't going to let me in it was so early. Then he saw I had a handful of money.

JONAS. Thank you. You didn't need to...

STEPHEN. I used half of that big money I made. So don't rough it up. Keep it in that box if you're not using it. Do you hear me?

JONAS. Yes sir.

STEPHEN. Well, put it on. It's meant to be worn.

> (**JONAS** *puts on the hat.*)

Looks good on you. You look like a real gentleman. That's what you want.

JONAS. Yes. I reckon.

STEPHEN. *(Re: hat.)* Didn't think I'd have a chance to give it you.

> (**STEPHEN** *pulls a small bottle of rum from his pocket.*)

Have some rum with me.

> (**JONAS** *hesitates.*)

JONAS. Papa.

STEPHEN. Have some rum! Imported from Jamaica! Drink! Don't make me twist your arm.

> *(They both drink.* **JONAS** *coughs.)*

You remember how I showed you to use your elbow when somebody tries to pick pocket? *(Demonstrates.)* Right in the ribs. Twice. The second time might break his bone, but you want that. If he has a knife or pick –

JONAS. Papa –

STEPHEN. Your mother's coming back. That's why I have to stay. If she comes back and doesn't find us... I got to stay. She's coming back.

JONAS. She's not coming back. She's not.

STEPHEN. I knew her! You didn't. She had fight. She had gumption. Whoever kidnapped her was in for a ride. She was no pansy. She probably fought him the whole way there, wherever he took her. And she's still fighting. I knew her. I loved her. She's fighting until she can break free and come back to us.

JONAS. That was over twenty years ago, Papa...

STEPHEN. So what! You wouldn't want somebody to wait for you? Somebody kidnap you from the people and place you know and you wouldn't want them to wait?

JONAS. No. I would want them to move on, like the world moves on.

STEPHEN. Well, that's the difference between you and me. There's no moving on without the ones you love. The ones you live for.

JONAS. Things change every day, Papa. You can't hold on to anything if it's changing.

STEPHEN. She's coming back to me and I'm gonna wait for her, if I have to die doing it. I will hold on until I die, Jonas.

(**JONAS** *pulls out a rolled up piece of paper.*)

JONAS. This is for you.

STEPHEN. I don't want anything.

JONAS. Open it.

STEPHEN. *(Opens. It's a drawing.)* What is this?

JONAS. It's Seneca. That's the bluffs. Two of the cemeteries. I couldn't fit the third. That's all the houses. The shanties on the bluff. Those are the mosquitoes and the churches and the school. Those are the pigs too. Running. That right there is our house. And that's you. Waving. That's me. Waving back.

(**STEPHEN** *looks at it. Overwhelmed.*)

Leave with me, Papa.

(Long silence.)

Thanks for the hat.

(He tries to hug him, but **STEPHEN** *pushes away.* **JONAS** *exits, looking back at* **STEPHEN**.*)*

STEPHEN. I can't leave, Jonas! Your mother's going to make her way back.

Scene Ten

(Van Cleef house. The next morning.)

*(**STEPHEN** stands on ladder. He lays down a large tin panel on his roof. He hums "Drinks to Me Only with Thine Eyes." **MATHIUS** walks up, holding his club. Nervous.)*

MATHIUS. Guten Morgen, Mister Van Cleef. How's the roof? Still unsteady for you?

STEPHEN. Oh, this roof is going to live long. Keep out rain, snow. Just had to find the strongest piece of tin. Going to start building another story onto the house tomorrow, with an even steadier roof. Then I'll feel protected and I can sleep in peace for the rest of my life. *(Then.)* What did I say about surprises and visitors?

MATHIUS. I don't recall. So many things to remember with you.

*(**STEPHEN** steps down from ladder, picks up a knife.)*

STEPHEN. I said shout your greeting before you show your face, or you might get knived.

(A beat, then.)

MATHIUS. You're up early, Mister Van Cleef.

STEPHEN. I feel like the only man in the world this time of the day, Mathius. Got to get up early for that. Meet the sun face-on. I could take on New York City with this feeling.

MATHIUS. And there you are again with the singing.

STEPHEN. Yes. Here I am a-gain. With a song that brings me joy.

(Then.)

MATHIUS. Were you able to go to the River for oysters this morning? There was a full moon. Must have made for a nice tide. Must have made for a large bed of oysters.

STEPHEN. Since you mention it, that full moon did its best dance ever last night. Found me an oystah as large as both hands.

> (**STEPHEN** *goes to a basket, puts down knife and pulls it out, shoves into* **MATHIUS**' *face.)*

There you are. Both hands! Never seen anything like it!

MATHIUS. It's a fine oyster. *(Trying sincerity.)* You're good at what you do.

STEPHEN. *(Correcting him.)* Oystahs.

MATHIUS. Pardon?

STEPHEN. They're called oystahs. If you're going to live in this city say it they way we say it. Oystahs. If you can't do that, you have no business living here.

> *(A slight pause.)*

MATHIUS. This is very difficult for me, Mister Van Cleef.

STEPHEN. What is difficult? You're a copper. You have a new uniform. Nothing needs to be difficult for you.

MATHIUS. This. Moment. It's –

STEPHEN. I've always believed a good song in the morning makes anything easy. Try singing. I can offer you lessons, but time doesn't permit such indulgence.

MATHIUS. Don't make me do this.

STEPHEN. You're going to clobber me over the head, Mathius? Watch me bleed to death? Piss on my body after? Why don't you try gutting me too. I'm certain that'll give a copper a whole lot of pleasure.

MATHIUS. It is time for you to leave. *(Coughs a little.)*

STEPHEN. Ha! Looks like you still have that cough. Told you before, you've got to be careful up here with the swamps and that Reservoir. They can be a working man's worse enemy. And that white plague will sneak up on you fast and knock you down into your grave even faster. But you don't listen to me. And I'm supposed to be just like your father.

MATHIUS. You must leave. You leave, the others will follow. No harm to you or them.

STEPHEN. Would you like some of this oystah, Mathius? I can sprinkle some salt and vinegar on it. It's real tasty.

MATHIUS. *(Frustrated.)* You can't live here. You must leave! You must leave, Mister Van Cleef!!

STEPHEN. Is that what they said to you before you left Württemberg?

MATHIUS. I don't understand.

STEPHEN. Before you left Württemberg! Did they say to you that you must leave your home?

MATHIUS. There was no work. Not enough wages for food or clothes. I can't talk of this now...

STEPHEN. But there is work here. I have wages for food and clothes. I even have a home.

MATHIUS. Mister Van Cleef, the other coppers are waiting out on Eighth Avenue...

STEPHEN. *(Continuing his rant.)* So the messenger has come here on his own volition? To spare me by kicking a man off his land. Is that why you crossed the Atlantic Ocean, Mathius? Stuffed into a ship of rats and filth and puke so one day you could make somebody leave the only thing that matters to them?

MATHIUS. I'm doing my job. I have to do what I'm told.

STEPHEN. You're doing what you think you have to do, because you're bloody dumb. The city preys on the bloody dumb.

MATHIUS. They city owns this land now. It will be the Central Park.

STEPHEN. I own this lot! I built this house! I've lost everything else so it's all I have left.

(**MATHIUS** *takes one step toward* **STEPHEN**.)

MATHIUS. I don't want to force. *(Sincere.)* Please don't make me force.

STEPHEN. This is my city! Do you hear me? My father helped pave Bloomingdale Road. Walked around with a limp after another man dropped a hack into his foot. His grandfather laid down the cobble on Wall Street.

MATHIUS. Mister Van Cleef –

STEPHEN. The father before that loaded sugar cane off those docks on Water Street. He dropped dead the day before New York finally freed its slaves. My great-grandmother provided water to the black men who built Trinity Church. A Lenape Indian she was. Every day she did this and they barely paid her a coin to buy bread. And what do we get for it? Riots and meanness. Whites and Irish burning up our homes, not letting us ride the same hawsecahs. Dragging us into the street at whim and kicking us dead if the notion hits them. This city doesn't like Blacks and we have the wounds to prove it. I'm staying here for them! Every one of them!

MATHIUS. Stephen. You have two choices.

STEPHEN. No! You have two choices! Either step out of my way or get knocked down.

MATHIUS. Zum Teufel! It's either me or those coppers waiting.

STEPHEN. I will not move a-gain. So you do what you have to do.

> (**STEPHEN** *begins to sing "Drink to Me" defiantly.* **MATHIUS,** *torn emotionally, turns around, then circles back. There's an intense struggle between the two men, then* **MATHIUS** *manages to break away and lifts up his club to an impenetrable* **STEPHEN.**)

End of Play

www.ingramcontent.com/pod-product-compliance
Lightning Source LLC
Chambersburg PA
CBHW070642120726
47909CB00004B/1550